P9-CDL-737

Failure to return
Library Material
is a crime —
N.C. General
Statutes # 14-398

Four Seasons in One Day

In her room, Isabelle lies sleeping. When she wakes up, she'll go on an incredible journey with her apple tree and her puppy, travelling through four seasons in just one day.

Follow her and see spring blossom, feel the summer's heat, gather in the autumn harvest and gasp at the cold of winter. But that's not all. **You can hear music for every season, too!**

Press the musical note on each page and listen as Vivaldi's *The Four Seasons* brings the story to life.

Quick! The little girl is stirring. Outside, birds are gathering, singing their hearts out in the morning sun. That they've returned can only mean one thing...

Spring is here.

PRESS HERE

Pender County Public Library
Hampstead Branch
Hampstead, NC 28443

PRESS HERE

After listening to the spring dawn chorus over breakfast, Isabelle fetches her apple tree and her bag.

"Come on, Pickle!" she calls to her puppy.

"We have to hurry to get to the Spring Festival by noon."

But as they leave the house, clouds fill the sky. Spring skies are as changeable as the wind... and full of sudden showers!

The rain has vanished by the time Isabelle and Pickle get to the Spring Festival at noon. Everywhere they look there are people smiling, dancing and laughing under the blue sky and shining sun. The air feels fresh and new, and lambs bleat and chicks tweet as everyone gathers to wear spring flowers, and plant vegetables.

An Easter Egg Hunt is underway.

"Come on, Pickle," says Isabelle. "Let's join in!"

PRESS HERE

As the afternoon wears on, it grows
hotter and hotter. The strong summer sun beats down
on the festival-goers, including Isabelle and Pickle. The heat tickles
their backs, prickles their skin and breathes down their necks.
The only thing they can do is close their eyes. But while they do so,
dark clouds appear from nowhere, covering the sun.
Too late, Isabelle awakens, and looks up at the dark sky...

PRESS HERE

The clouds rumble angrily and, with a blast of lightning, the sky cracks open! A second later, rain tumbles down.

"Quick, Pickle," shouts Isabelle. "Run!"

PRESS HERE

After a while, the storm fades, and
a breeze stirs the air. Everyone sighs with relief.
It's time to collect in the autumn harvest!

There are shiny red apples, crunchy orange carrots and
soft, golden hay. Isabelle and Pickle help everyone gather
food for the winter, picking apples off their own tree.
Around them, animals do their own harvesting, too.

PRESS HERE

In the fading light,
the air becomes cooler.
The leaves turn orange, red
and brown, and fall from the
trees in huge, dusty piles.
"Let's jump through them as we
walk back, Pickle!" cries Isabelle.
Above them the birds fly away
to warmer lands, and all
around animals prepare
for a long, cold winter.

Isabelle and Pickle
aren't far from their
house when the snow
comes. The winter cold bites
into their hands and faces,
making them shiver and tingle.
They run around to keep warm,
then build a handsome snowman,
with stones for eyes and a
carrot for a nose.
"I'm freezing!" says Isabelle
when it's finished.

PRESS HERE

"The sun's setting!" says Isabelle.
"Hurry, Pickle. We've got to get inside
before it gets dark."

They run along as fast as they can, but Isabelle
stumbles on an icy bit of path. She trips, slips, and the
apple tree falls out of her hands, rolls down a hill and
into a stream, where the pot smashes!

"My poor tree," says Isabelle as she sits at home, safe and sound.

"I'm so sad I lost it. What's the matter, Pickle?" The puppy is scratching at Isabelle's pocket. Isabelle puts her hand in and finds an apple. "You're so clever!" she exclaims. Because, after she has eaten the apple, she is left with the core, which has a few brown glossy seeds. The perfect seeds to plant for spring, so a new apple tree can grow.

PRESS HERE

Antonio Vivaldi

Antonio Vivaldi was born in Venice, Italy in 1678. He had bright red hair (although he often wore a wig on top of it, like most men in those days). His dad taught him the violin, and he went on to become a very famous composer, writing more than 800 pieces of music.

One of his most famous pieces is The Four Seasons, which was composed in 1723. Vivaldi was inspired by his friend Marco Ricci, who painted pictures of the seasons, to write pieces of music that sounded like spring, summer, autumn and winter.

The Four Seasons is an example of program music. This is what musicians call music that paints a picture in your head. Vivaldi managed to make a small group of stringed instruments sound like lots of different things. Along with all that, he wrote some very good tunes that you could whistle if you tried. Have a listen to the music on the next page, and see what sounds you can hear, and what tunes you can hum or whistle. The story in this book is inspired by The Four Seasons, but you might think the music tells a different tale!

GLOSSARY

Rhythm – the beat of a piece of music

Phrase – a group of notes that are part of a longer piece of music

Orchestra – a group of instruments that play together

Key – this tells the musicians what special notes to play. Major keys sound happy and minor keys sound sad.

Trills – moving quickly from a note to the one next to it and back again

Solo – when one instrument plays on its own

First published in Great Britain and the USA in 2016 by
Frances Lincoln Children's Books, 74-77 White Lion Street, London N1 9PF

Visit our blogs at QuartoKnows.com
QuartoKnows.com

The Story Orchestra: Four Seasons in One Day copyright
© Frances Lincoln Limited 2016

Illustrations copyright © Jessica Courtney-Tickle 2016

All rights reserved.

ISBN 978-1-84780-877-6

Written by Katie Cotton with notes by Katy Flint • Designed by Andrew Watson
Published by Rachel Williams • Production by Jenny Cundill

Printed in China

1 3 5 7 9 8 6 4 2

Clips taken from recording copyright © John Harrison, violin, with Robert Turizziani
conducting the Wichita State University Chamber Players. Live, unedited performance
at the Wiedemann Recital Hall, Wichita State University, 6 February 2000

These clips have been edited for this book format

Music by Antonio Vivaldi composed 1723 and published in 1725